Engagement in Stickleback Hollow

The Mysteries of Stickleback Hollow®

By C.S. Woolley

A Mightier Than the Sword UK Publication

©2023

Engagement in Stickleback Hollow

The Mysteries of Stickleback Hollow®

By C. S. Woolley

A Mightier Than the Sword UK Publication

Paperback Edition

ISBN Paperback 978-1-99-117193-1

ISBN Hardback 978-1-99-117195-5

ISBN Kindle 978-1-7386037-9-4

Cover Design by Get Covers

The Mysteries of Stickleback Hollow® is a Registered Trademark 1235153

For

Victoria and Nick

Congratulations on your engagement

Author's Note

Thanks for taking the time to read *Engagement in Stickleback Hollow*, I hope you like the book. For those of you who are just diving into the series, the year is 1841 and a lot has happened to get us to this point.

We have met a great many faces up to this point, and with the celebration of Lady Sarah's engagement, we shall see a lot of them again. Some will be characters that we have seen many times, other that have only appeared once or twice, but they are all coming out to celebrate.

As this engagement has also been a long time coming, I hope that you found it to be an acceptable match for her ladyship. There will be some who may have wanted her to end up with one of the other suitors she had, but the story has always been destined for these two to end up together. But never fear, there will be happy endings for those who were unsuccessful in securing her hand, and they will not be gone from Stickleback Hollow either.

I would like to also say a huge congratulations to Victoria and Nick on their recent engagement. Victoria is the daughter of a very dear friend, and after everything their family has been through in the recent months, they deserve a time of joy.

Finally, to all of those that are celebrating a recent engagement, I would like to offer you the most heartfelt congratulations, and wish you ever happiness.

Kia Kaha.

The Characters

Lady Sarah Montgomery Baird Watson-Wentworth

The heroine

Brigadier George Webb-Kneelingroach

Lord of Grangeback and Lady Sarah's Guardian

Bosworth

The butler

Mrs Bosworth

The housekeeper

Cooky

The cook

Mr Alexander Hunter

A huntsman and groundskeeper of Grangeback

Pattinson

An Akita, Alexander's hunting dog

Constable Arwyn Evans

Policeman in Stickleback Hollow

Doctor Jack Hales

The doctor in Stickleback Hollow

Miss Angela Baker

Seamstress and mother of the Baker boys

Stanley Baker

Son of Miss Baker

Lee Baker

Son of Miss Baker

Reverend Percy Butterfield

The vicar in Stickleback Hollow

Mr Thomas Egerton

Son of Wilbraham & Elizabeth

Mr Edward Christopher Egerton

Son of Wilbraham & Elizabeth

Mr Richard Hales

Son of Doctor Hales

Mr Oliver Henry Brown

An American Gentleman, Cousin to the Egerton Family

Sylvia

Lady Sarah's Companion and Lady's Maid.

Lady Szonja, Countess of Huntingdon

Cousin of the Egertons, Ally of Lady Sarah

Constable Thompson Buckley

A constable of Stickleback Hollow

Baron Christian Friedrich Freiherr von Stockmar

Advisor to Queen Victoria from the Court of King Leopold

Arthur Wellesley, Duke of Wellington

Hero of the Napoleonic Wars, Politician

Charles Arbuthnot

Former Ambassador, friend to the Duke of Wellington

Wilson

The innkeeper in Stickleback Hollow

Mrs Emma Wilson

Wife of Wilson and cook at the inn

Reverend Percy Butterfield

The vicar in Stickleback Hollow

The Honourable Mr Wilbraham Egerton

Owner of Tatton Park

Mrs Elizabeth Egerton nee Sykes

Wife of Wilbraham

Mrs Charlotte Egerton nee Milner

Wife of Thomas

Mrs Mary Egerton nee Pierrepont

Fiancée of Edward

Mr Harry Taylor

A gentleman in the employment of John Smith

Mr James Christian

A retired missionary

Miss Gunn

A retired governess

Mrs Claydon nee Beaumont

A governess

Mr Mitchell Claydon

An explorer

Chapter 1

Celebrations are one of the most precious parts of life, and for the Brigadier George Webb-Kneelingroach there could be no greater event to celebrate than this.

His son, Mr Alexander Hunter Webb-Kneelingroach, and his ward, Lady Sarah Montgomery Baird Watson Wentworth, were finally engaged. It was not the first engagement that the pair had made, but he hoped that it would be the last.

There had been strife, disaster, and heartbreak that had littered their courtship, other suitors that had done their best to woo the lady, but her heart belong to Alex, and it was something of a great relief for the brigadier.

It had been months of waiting for the lady to provide Mr Hunter with an answer, as he had not been the only man to propose to her, and the pain of how their previous engagement had ended, had served to burden her mind and heart with doubt.

But her love for him had overcome all of the doubts and reservations she had, and now they could finally put their past behind them, and move forward together towards their future as husband and wife.

The household of Grangeback Estate, the manor that belonged to the brigadier, had been overjoyed by the news. The servants had known Alexander since he was a young boy, and all adored Lady Sarah.

To have the co-heirs to the estate marrying also meant that the future of Grangeback was secured, something that lifted the worries of more than one of the employees of the household.

Sylvia, Lady Sarah's companion and lady's maid, was the only member of the household who was not thrilled by the news. It was not that she wanted Lady Sarah not to marry, or that she thought there was a better prospect for her ladyship, but because she did not trust Mr Hunter.

He had broken her heart once before, and she was all but certain he would break it again. But she did not voice this opinion. She kept the thought to herself, but had decided to watch out for Mr Hunter doing even the smallest thing that might hurt her mistress and ensure that she could limit the damage.

"I have sent a telegraph to The Times to announce our happy news for all to see. Once it is in print, I am sure that we will have all manner of questions to answer about the wedding, but before any decisions are made about your nuptials, we should celebrate your engagement," the brigadier told the happy couple as Bosworth the butler poured champagne for the brigadier, Lady Sarah, Mr Hunter and Sylvia.

"Does this mean that you are going to host a ball?" Lee Baker asked. Lee and Stanley Baker were two young boys on the verge of manhood, who had been apprenticed to Lady Sarah to learn about solving mysteries. They were orphans that had been adopted as doorstep babies by Miss Angela Baker, the local seamstress, and she had ensured that the boys both knew how to sew and tailor before they had been able to walk.

Their apprenticeship had been something of their own creation, and Miss Baker had agreed to such a thing because the boys could learn a great deal of skill working in the great house, so when it was clear that solving mysteries was not a career path that could feed them, the boys would have more than one trade that the would be able to fall back on.

They were both two young to drink, but they were not excluded from the celebration because of it.

"Yes, I think that is a most splendid idea,"

Lady Sarah agreed.

"Who should we invite?" Mr Hunter asked, sounding less than enthusiastic about the prospect of such a party.

"Only those that we would want to attend the wedding. To have those who we will not invite attend the ball will only lead to uncomfortable situations later," Lady Sarah replied.

"Then we should start on the guest list at once! Sylvia, dear would you mind acting as our secretary?" the brigadier asked as he rummaged around in his desk for paper and a quill.

He enjoyed writing with quills more than pens and subsequently there were quills hidden in practically every drawer in the house.

"Very well," Sylvia agreed with a sigh and began to write the names of those that Lady Sarah, Mr Hunter and the brigadier suggested without the others contradicting them.

Once the list of all the friends and family of the happy couple had been made, Sylvia was tasked with writing invitations to the engagement ball. As she wrote the cards, she wondered what become of her after the wedding.

The brigadier had promised her that she would remain as part of the household and always have a home at Grangeback, something that had yet to be tested. Had Grace Read, Lady Sarah's previous maid, been rescued from the men who had kidnapped her , and not murdered, then Sylvia was not so certain she would have had a place within the house.

Assurances had been made to her, but those were merely words, as far as she was concerned, and they had never been tested. But she also feared the answer. Lady Sarah had met Sylvia when the pair had been taken from the hospital and a mad doctor and nurse were set on punishing fallen women. The pair had been stopped, but whereas Lady Sarah had been welcomed home, Sylvia had found herself on the streets.

It was there, before Christmas, that Lady Sarah had found her and brought her into the Grangeback family, something that Sylvia would always be grateful for. She knew full well that she would have died on those cold streets of Chester, and that she would not have been mourned.

What she feared most of all was finding herself cast out and living on the streets once more, and in her mind there were so many reasons that she might be summarily dismissed from service.

She tried her best to focus on the invitations, and dismiss the negative thoughts that threatened to overwhelm her brain, but the more she fought against them, the more they came.

She considered writing her letter of resignation and leaving the house on her own terms, but equally, she had nowhere to go, and no one she could prevail upon.

By the time she had finished the

invitations, Sylvia had concluded that she would have to wait and see what the future brought, and hope that when the wedding finally did take place, she would still have a home within the manor walls.

The date was set for the ball just three weeks after the engagement announcement appeared in The Times. Sylvia had been quick writing the invitations, and they had been sent out with all speed to their guests. Most received their invitations to the ball not long after they had read the announcement in the newspaper, though there were a small number of guests who had read their invitations before the morning paper, but nearly all were surprised and delighted to learn of the happy news.

Only Mr Oliver Henry Brown was not thrilled to be invited to the ball. He had been Lady Sarah's other suitor, and almost certain that she would choose him over Mr Hunter. But he had also promised her ladyship that no matter what her decision, he would remain a great and dedicated friend to her.

He received the invitation to the ball first, as he was the closest neighbour to Grangeback, and though there would be a great many people invited from the village of Stickleback Hollow that lay between the two great houses, it was a common courtesy that the lords in their manors were given invitations before the common folk.

Oliver had no reason to feel surprised at

seeing the invitation, he had known when he was turned down that Lady Sarah had chosen Mr Hunter, and that the two would be married, but he had not expected to feel so much pain at seeing such an invitation in black and white.

Part of his heart had hoped that Lady Sarah would change her mind, but he had scolded himself for such hope. For her to break her engagement a second time and run to him was not only a complete fantasy, but involved the destruction of the happiness of others for the sake of his own vanity.

The invitation sat upon the desk in his study, staring at him, daring him to decline, but rather than do so, he picked up his pen and wrote his reply accepting, and sent his butler to deliver his response in person.

It was only 10 o'clock in the morning, but the gentleman strode over to where a decanter of bourbon sat and poured himself a glass. Once he had drained it, he poured himself another.

He moved over to the chair that sat before a blazing hearth and nursed the second glass as he stared into the flames and wondered where he should remain in England, or whether the time was right for him to return to America.

Chapter 2

To say that the ball was a grand affair would be to understate the expense to which the brigadier and the people of Stickleback Hollow went to in order to celebrate the upcoming marriage of their favourite son and daughter of the village.

Miss Baker had her seamstress skills put to the test with dresses for Lady Sarah and Sylvia for the ball, as well as the new coats for the brigadier and Mr Hunter. With Miss Baker occupied and unable to make the dresses for everyone in the village, those that wanted new clothes for the ball had made a journey to Chester in search of fine yet affordable clothing.

Most wanted to look presentable rather than gaudy, though there were a handful of ladies that were no possessed of fine taste, and found cheap shops that sold dresses that would have been better in a concert hall than a ball.

Cooky and Mrs Bosworth had both decreed that the ball would be finer than anything that anyone had ever seen in Stickleback Hollow, even more so than the Christmas dinners that were held at the manor.

There was not a great deal of time to plan for the ball, but the two women worked quickly, and enlisted the help of people throughout the village to make the event special.

Mr and Mrs Claydon were both grateful to the brigadier for allowing them to use

Grangeback Manor for their wedding reception, and so threw their full support behind the event, Mrs Claydon often going above and beyond the call of duty.

The two had been on a honeymoon to Scotland and the wild highlands with the beauty views of lochs and mountains. It was not the exotic wilds that Mr Claydon had often explored in his career, but it was the perfect place for the pair to be alone and celebrate the start of their new life together.

They had returned and begun life in he village in earnest, starting by finding a new companion for Miss Gunn, primarily because Mr Claydon did not wish to have two women for the price of one in his house.

The girl was a good sort that they had

found, pleasant enough with no real vices to speak of and Miss Gunn seemed to find her society tolerable.

Mrs Claydon had worried about how she would fill her time now that she was freed of caring for Miss Gunn, but the engagement ball had given her plenty of purpose, and the thought of the future that the union between Lady Sarah and Mr Hunter Webb-Kneelingroach provided for the village was one that made Mrs Claydon certain that there would be plenty for her to do.

A feast was prepared that was contributed to by every person in the village. Emma from Wilson's Inn had prepared a fine selection of pies, both sweet and savoury, to be served. Mr Pick, the greengrocer, had his wife create salads and roasted vegetable dishes that had been in the family cookbook for generations. Even the Reverend Percy Butterfield provided several bottles of homemade wine for the occasion.

Though the connection between Lady Sarah and the Royal Family was now quite well-known in the village, none expected a visit from the queen and her prince, but the nor did they expect some of the guests who did arrive for the ball.

The Evans family had come from Wales to attend the ball, and were all staying at the manor. Edryd was once more the jolly figure he had been before the terrible events that had taken place at their farm. Bronwyn had recovered well, and with almost no residual damage from the beating she had received.

There was some limited movement in her wrist, and pain in her knees, but she was a tough woman who used them as a reminder of what she had survived. Edryd often insisted that she did less, but Bronwyn had not slowed down or reduced her duties on the farm one jot.

Derwyn Evans was far less vibrant a personality than he had been previously, and it was understandable since his fiancée, Miss DeVille, had not survived their last encounter in quite such good condition as his mother.

Her constitution was a good deal weaker and she was often taken ill from the smallest affliction. She walked with a stick on most occasions, and a chair had been acquired for her on the times when her body could not bring itself to walk.

Bronwyn had talked about hiring a nurse for her, but Derwyn had insisted that the family take care of her, but as her health seemed determined to not improve, the time was coming when a nurse would be forced upon Derwyn, whether he wanted his intended to have one or not.

Mr Oliver Henry Brown was the first guest to arrive, and the brigadier was most taken aback by his eagerness to attend the event.

George was worried that there might be some unpleasantness, but was relieved when Mr Brown shock Mr Hunter's hand in friendship and kissed the bride-to-be's hand.

"That was unexpectedly gallant of you,"

Sylvia said with surprise as Mr Brown approached her. The pair were the only people at the manor with nothing to do whilst they waited for the guests to arrive.

"I made a promise to her ladyship. That if I were not the man she chose, I would still be pledged to her in friendship. Not coming tonight and supporting her choice would not be very friendly," Mr Brown replied with a shrug.

"Perhaps, but it would have saved you some measure of pain, surely?" Sylvia said with apparent concern.

"Pain comes and goes. In twenty years, we will all look back on this and laugh at the folly of youth," Mr Brown attempted a wry smile, but it changed to more of a wince as he watched Lady Sarah placing her hand on Mr

Hunter's arm.

"Pain does more damage than we give it credit for. Do not stay if it is too much to bear. In fact, come, let us go to the patio. There are a number of drinks there and the crochet lawn is set. Perhaps we can distract you with a game and a glass," Sylvia said kindly.

"You have never been this nice to anyone before, save for her ladyship. Why are you doing this for me?" Mr Brown asked with confusion.

"Because the three of you were locked in an untenable situation. There was no way that everyone could be happy, and I know that Lady Sarah regrets how much this has hurt you. Besides, I could never be cruel to a wounded animal. So, accept the kindness, do not think too much on where it comes from or why you are receiving it. Just be grateful for the distraction," Sylvia said firmly and led Mr Brown outside.

Sylvia knew the pair would not be missed, and was certain that if they were to disappear until breakfast the next day, not a soul would notice.

Not long after Mr Brown's arrival, Doctor Jack Hales, and his son, Richard Hales, arrived. They were greeted warmly and told that Sylvia and Mr Brown were in the ballroom. This led to a great deal of confusion for the pair when they entered the grand room and found that the two were nowhere insight. But the sound of the crochet mallet on ball soon told them where their friends were hiding.

The musicians that were hired to play for the ball were in attendance, but would not begin playing until much later in the evening.

As more of the village arrived, the ballroom began to fill with people, but more than half of them soon drifted outside to join the fun on the patio, especially when the more elevated guests began to arrive.

The brigadier had invited many of his friends from his army days, as well as those who had been friendly with Lady Sarah's father. They arrived in large groups, and began to make the hall feel very stiff and formal. The Egertons arrived with one such group, and though Thomas and Edward could see the fun on the patio, they had to wait a full hour before they could excuse themselves from their company, leaving their wives to talk with other women, to join Richard, Sylvia and their cousin outside.

Pattinson had been let out in the gardens for the night, Mrs Bosworth had declared it was not proper for dogs to attend a ball, and so he too had found his way to the patio, and Sylvia's side.

Countess Szjona arrived separately from the Egertons, which had surprised the brigadier, but only until he saw who was accompanying her.

Baron Christian von Stockmar had volunteered to attend the ball and represent the royal household at the event, with assurances that Queen Victoria and Prince Albert would attend their wedding. He had been invited in his own right, but he carried with him the royal seal and a letter from the queen.

He had not wished to arrive alone, and the Countess Szonja was a suitable companion for him, especially as she too would be arriving without a companion.

Captain Charles Robert Finlay arrived not long after the baron and countess. He carried with him a letter from Lady de Mandeville expressing her delight and best wishes, as well as her apologies that she could not attend.

The final group of guests to arrive were by far the most distinguished and Lady Sarah was quite surprised that they had chosen to attend, much less arrived together.

The Duke and Duchess of Cambridge had met Lady Sarah on no less than three occasions and were both very found of her. There was no relation between them, as they belonged to a different branch of the queen's family to Lady Sarah, but they felt as though Lady Sarah should have been family to them, and as such had decided to attend.

They bore notes and well-wishes from the rest of their family for the happy couple, and had brought with them two other friends.

The Duke of Wellington and Charles Arbuthnot had been in no doubt that they would attend the ball to celebrate the engagement of Lady Sarah and Mr Hunter. Charles was a great admirer of Lady Sarah and though the duke was as well, he felt more kinship with Mr Hunter and his direct attitude to life, as well as his disdain for useless people.

The only two faces that seemed to be missing from the ball were Arwyn Evans and Thompson Buckley, the village policemen, but rather than be announced as guests, the pair had come through the gardens and simply merged with the crowd on the crochet lawn.

The villagers on the patio all left their delights of fun and homemade wine when the call for dinner was made and they all made their way to the great banquet hall, finding themselves quite taken aback when they saw the Duke of Wellington as well as the Duke and Duchess of Cambridge.

There were no speeches planned for the occasion, but the two dukes could not let the evening pass without remarks being made. They had discussed at length on the journey to

Grangeback Manor the order in which they should speak. They had both agreed that if the brigadier rose then they would speak after him, first the Duke of Cambridge, then the Duke of Wellington. If he did not, they would speak in the same order anyway.

Before the meal was served, the two waited a moment to see if the brigadier would speak, and when he did not, the Duke of Cambridge rose and with the slight chiming of knife on crystal for silence, he gave an eloquent speech, extolling not only the virtues of the couple but of the estate of marriage.

When he was finished, the Arthur Wellesley rose and clearing his throat, he said,

"Many of you are more accustomed to me giving orders than making grand speeches, and

I cannot speak as eloquently as our dear friend can."

His remarks were met with laughter and slight applause from the old soldiers in the room.

"But I can speak to the subject of character, and how both the bride-to-be and groom-to-be are such characters that I was certain were gone from this world. They are both self-sacrificing people, not just towards the other, or their family and friends, but perfect strangers who find themselves in distress. They are warm, caring, but not foolish people. In fact, I would like to meet an individual who could out fox the pair of them. We have seen many try and fail, after all."

This time the laughter came from the

friends of the couple and the villagers.

"I know that they well have a happy future together, one that will be filled with mystery, danger, and more trouble than most of us will ever see in a lifetime. I also know that there is no other life better suited for them. To her ladyship and her lord, may they be very happy together."

The room rose to their feet at the last comment and raised their glasses and echoed "Her ladyship and her lord."

The food was then brought into the hall. To save the servants of the manor from missing out on the meal, only Cooky had remained in the kitchen until the food was ready. Footmen and kitchen maids had been brought from Tatton Park and Duffleton Hall to help serve the food and prepare it.

Once her part was done, Cooky had left the kitchen to join the party, just in time to here the speeches.

She had outdone herself in her preparations from the kitchen. With so many guests it had seemed that the brigadier had considered three courses appropriate, but Cooky had prepared seven.

Each was more delicious than the last, and she glowed with pride at the reception her food received.

The menu began with raw oysters, three per guest, on silver platters, followed by a vegetable soup that was not too heavy or light either. Smoked haddock with mustard and herring with cucumber sauce were then served to the guests. The fourth course of the evening was venison, roasted potatoes and Mrs Pick's roasted vegetables. Next came the Mrs Pick's salad, all of which were eaten with great gusto. None of the plates were sent back with food on them.

Raspberry summer pudding and candied pears was what Cooky knew to be her crowing achievement of the meal. But as the dessert was being served, one of the footman whispered to Lady Sarah and she had to excuse herself to speak with a messenger.

The messenger stood stiffly in the hallway, he had refused to relinquish his missive as he had strict instructions that it was to be passed to Lady Sarah's hands only.

She took the piece of paper from the

gloved hands of the messenger and unrolled it. The message simply read,

Congratulations, may you get all you truly deserve.

There was nothing more. It was not even signed. When her ladyship looked up from the letter, the messenger had already left. She read the letter a second time and then placed it on the table in the hall.

She was slightly confused by such a message seeming to be so urgent that only she could receive it, but she tried to put it out of her mind as she returned to her meal.

The raspberry summer pudding and candied pears were delicious, but halfway through her dessert, Lady Sarah began to feel quite dizzy.

"What is it?" Mr Hunter asked with worry as he noticed her struggling to eat. Before she could answer, Lady Sarah collapsed on the table.

The doctor was on his feet and running to her ladyship before most people in the hall knew anything was wrong.

Captain Finlay rushed out to the stables and order a carriage with the fastest horses be prepared at once and brought to the front of the house. He dashed back to the banqueting hall to find the doctor announcing.

"She has been poisoned. There is not much time, hurry."

Mr Hunter picked up his fiancée in his

arms and strode out of the banqueting hall with Captain Finlay and the doctor on either side.

"The carriage should be ready now. We will both go with you," Captain Finlay said as they marched quickly. Mr Hunter did not say a word, instead he bit down on his lip and prayed that they would not be too late.

"The hospital and quickly," the doctor shouted to the driver as the three men climbed into the carriage, Mr Hunter keeping his arms wrapped tightly about Lady Sarah.

None of them protested as Pattinson came charging around the house and leapt in before the door was closed. The Akita licked his mistress' hand and whined, looking up at Mr Hunter with helpless eyes.

The guests in the banqueting hall were

left stunned, no more so than poor Cooky, who had burst into tears.

"Ladies and gentlemen, if we could all please remain calm, and the hall be left exactly as it is. The brigadier will lead us all to the ballroom where we can await news," Charles Arbuthnot said in his finest diplomatic voice.

No one argued about needing to leave or being held at the manor, not a person amongst their number seemed to consider the horrible possibility that one of them was responsible.

But the thought had occurred to more than just Charles Arbuthnot. As the guests filled out of the banqueting hall and the servants were instructed to not clear away anything further, Sylvia, Mr Brown, Arwyn, Constable Buckley, the Duke of Wellington, and

Richard Hales all watched the crowd looking for someone who might try to leave unnoticed.

Chapter 3

The journey to the hospital seemed endless, but the moment they arrived, the doctor sprang into action. Her ladyship was admitted immediately and Doctor Hales set to work doing all he could for her.

Captain Finlay, Mr Hunter and Pattinson were forced to wait in the hallway whilst the doctor worked and they could only catch glimpses of what was happening in the room when a nurse rushed in or out of it.

Alex's hand never left the collar of the dog as they stood there, as he knew that the moment he released the dog, he would charge into Lady Sarah's room and only be in the way.

After an hour of waiting, one of the nurses took pity on the pair and took them to a room where they could sit down until more news was known.

The waiting room was hardly comfortable, but it was a slight step above waiting in the hallway. The nurse offered them hot beverages, or something a little stronger, and though Captain Finlay accepted, Mr Hunter refused to touch anything until he knew more about Lady Sarah's condition.

Minutes stretched to hours, hours to days, as they waited for news. Captain Finlay did not speak a word as they sat. He did not want to distract Mr Hunter, but he was there for company, and Mr Hunter appreciated it more than he would ever be able to articulate.

Four hours passed before the doctor came to see them.

"She is stable for now," Doctor Hales sighed heavily.

"For now?" Mr Hunter asked with concern.

"I cannot say what is going to happen. She is strong. She has always been a fighter, as you know. But the poison has done a lot of damage," Doctor Hale said sadly.

"When will you know?" Captain Finlay asked.

"That I cannot say. It may be that she survives a few days, a few weeks, or just a few hours. Until she is awake,. and her strength is returned, then we will know she is fully out of danger," Jack Hales said sadly and placed a comforting hand on Mr Hunter's shoulder.

"Then I shall wait with her until she is awake and strong enough to survive this," Mr Hunter said flatly. The doctor made no argument and led Mr Hunter and Patterson to Lady Sarah's room.

Captain Finlay declined the invitation to join them for the moment.

"I will follow presently," he said. Instead, he made his way back through the hospital to the front entrance and spoke to the nurse at the counter.

"Might I trouble you for a pen and some paper?" he asked pleasantly.

"Of course," the nurse said, and hunted around until she found some stationery for him. He leant on the counter and began to write:

My dearest Margaret-Ann,

I bear ill tidings. There has been attack on our mutual friend. Poison, it seems. The doctor has done all he can for now. She is alive. But more than that, I cannot say.

I shall remain here to protect her from any further attempts should the poisoner decide that her survival is not acceptable. I would ask. But you bring all your considerable resources there in helping to unmask the villain in this case.

Your loyal and obedient servant.

Captain Charles Robert Finley

He folded the letter up and addressed it, then arranged for a messenger to carry the note to London where his employer maintained an office, and the dispatches for India for her were carried from.

The post was an inefficient way to send such messages, especially if one wanted them to arrive in a timely manner. Once he was assured the message was the way, he returned to Mr Hunter who sat Lady Sarah's side.

As he walked into the room, a large woman, clearly the matron, was objecting to the presence of Pattinson in the room.

"This is a hospital. No dogs are allowed in here. Utter nonsense to bring such a beast in here."

Pattinson was growling at the woman, clearly showing he understood what she was saying and did not like being referred to in such a manner.

"My dear lady, you cannot object to a guard dog when a woman has just been poisoned," Doctor Hales attempted to persuade the nurse.

"I can object to whatever I please. This is not sensible, to have a animal filled with disease in the hospital. Remove him at once," the matron said.

"No," Mr Hunter said flatly, his voice was monotone and mildly threatening. The matron was slightly taken a back a back by such a tone for the man who had shown absolutely no interest in speaking before that moment.

She was not used to having her authority questioned, even by doctors.

"My dear lady," Captain Finlay said. "Perhaps in these rather extraordinary circumstances, it might be best to at least allow the dog to remain, for now. If he does not leave the room, except to be taken outside to relieve himself, there can be no real health risks to other patients," Captain Finlay said in a voice to mollify the matron somewhat.

"And who is to take him outside?" the matron demanded.

"It will be my responsibility," Captain Finlay said firmly.

"That is very good of you to offer,". Doctor Hales noted appreciatively.

"I shall ensure that he takes all of his

comfort breaks outside. Vital staff know that you have here will not to be accosted," the captain said, speaking for both him and the dog.

"Very well, but the first sign of trouble, and both the dog and you will be out," the matron warned as she left the trio alone in Lady Sarah's room..

Pattinson's head rested upon the edge of the bed, next to where Mr Hunter he was leaning, his hands grasping Lady Sarah's. The two were extremely glad to see the back of the matron, but they both knew she would be back.

"A moment, if you please, captain," Jack said in a low voice. Charles nodded and followed Doctor Hales out into the corridor. "Will you stay the whole time?"

"I will," the captain said.

"Very good. Because it is highly likely she will not survive until morning. If that is the case, I would ask that you would be kind enough to take care of Mr Hunter. It has been a hard day for him," the doctor said, emotion causing his voice to crack.

"It has been a hard day for us all, doctor," Captain Finlay said kindly placing his hand on the doctor's shoulder.

"I know she means it means a great deal to everyone in Stickleback Hollow. It is not only Mr Hunter that this is hard on. I should talk to the brigadier, sooner rather than later. He will want to know what is going on, " the doctor sighed

"Very well, return to the village. We will both remain here, come back in the morning once you have rested and hopefully we shall have unexpectedly happy news," Captain Finlay said.

"I pray you are right," Doctor Hale said. "In all my years of being a physician. I have never wanted to be wrong more than I wish to be wrong now."

"Very good. I shall ensure things run smoothly here in your absence. Just make sure the matron stays far away from Mr Hunter. I am not sure that she will survive a second encounter with him," Captain Finlay said dryly, causing Doctor Hales to chuckle in spite of himself.

"No, indeed. *Doctor* Finlay," Doctor

Hales replied.

Chapter 4

Mr Hunter and the captain remained at the hospital with Pattinson that night, and the doctor returned to Stickleback Hollow to tell the brigadier the grim prognosis.

The journey to the manor gave Jack Hales time to imagine all the possible outcomes of the news he was about to break to one of his oldest friends, but he was not prepared for the sight that he was met with as he arrived at Grangeback.

All of the guests from the engagement dinner were still in attendance, and a great deal of police had been added to their number. Bosworth was stood on the steps of the house, eagerly looking out for the return of the doctor, Captain Finlay or Mr Hunter.

"Doctor!" Bosworth cried as the doctor's carriage pulled up and Jack pushed open the door.

"I bring news, Bosworth, of the gravest kind, where is your master?" the doctor asked hurriedly.

"He is in the ballroom with all his guests," Bosworth replied sadly.

"His guests?" the doctor frowned.

"No one has been inclined to leave. It has caused Cooky no small amount of stress as there are a good deal more mouths to feed than she was expecting," Bosworth said delicately.

"Is the chief constable here?" the doctor asked.

"Yes, he is," Bosworth confirmed.

"Good, can you ask the brigadier, Sylvia, Arwyn, the Baker boys, Richard and the chief constable to meet me in the brigadier's study?" the doctor asked.

"Very well," Bosworth said. But he hesitated for a moment, debating whether to ask the question he dreaded the answer to. "Doctor, will she live?"

"I do not know," Jack sighed and shook his head. Bosworth nodded and hurried as fast as his ageing legs would carry him to gather those the doctor wished to see.

The doctor did not have to wait long for Bosworth to summon his small audience to the study.

"Doctor, tell us, how fares my ward?" the brigadier asked desperately as the door to the study was closed.

"Poorly," Jack sighed and ran his fingers through his thinning hair. "Her ladyship teeters on the edge of life and death. If she is to survive the night, it will be nothing short of divine intervention from the hand of God. I have done all I can as a man of science, and there is nothing more that can be done."

"Except to pray," Richard said and all those present took a moment to silently pray for the miracle they needed.

"Where are Captain Finlay and Mr

Hunter Webb-Kneelingroach?" Captain Jonnes-Smith asked, breaking the silence.

"They are at the hospital, along with Pattinson. Captain Finlay has promised to protect her ladyship and Mr Hunter with the dog's help. I am sure that any further assistance your men can provide would be greatly appreciated," Jack said pointedly, and the chief constable nodded his agreement.

"It is for the best that Alexander remains with her, if he were not at the hospital, he would only want to investigate, and I must insist that this attempt on her ladyship's life be investigated by professionals," the chief constable said.

"Excuse me?" Sylvia asked with a look of disbelief.

"This is no time for amateur detectives to interfere," the chief constable said firmly and Richard had to place a firm hand on Sylvia's arm to keep her from pressing the issue.

Constable Evans shifted uncomfortably where he stood and tried to slip out of the room, but Stanley and Lee Baker were both blocking the door.

"We are not amateurs. We are detectives. We have learned from Lady Sarah. We can find her poisoner," the pair said in unison, which slightly unnerved the chief constable.

"I believe that Mr Arbuthnot will also have some objections to the police being solely responsible for such an investigation. He has a great deal of experience and connections that will be of great use to you," the brigadier said and began to usher Captain Jonnes-Smith from the room.

The Baker boys glared at the policeman as he passed them, but they stood aside and let him leave the room. When the door was closed behind the brigadier and chief constable, Sylvia turned to her friends,

"Tells us doctor, should we be looking for an attempted murderer who will strike again or a murderer who will be trying to escape?" she asked earnestly.

"An attempted murderer watching to see if they are a successful murderer," Jack replied thoughtfully.

"Then we should begin our own investigation now. Unless you will feel that you are being torn between two masters?" Richard asked, looking at Arwyn.

"Not at all. I doubt that the chief constable will include myself or Constable Buckley in the investigation, so we shall both be at your disposal," Constable Evans replied with a shrug.

"What about Mr Arbuthnot? Will he not be a valuable ally to help investigating?" Richard asked. He had not met the man before and only knew what he had been told by the others about him.

"I can almost guarantee he will be more of a hindrance than a help," Sylvia said, whilst chewing her bottom lip.

"Oh?" Arwyn frowned at her.

"He is from a world where he is seen as an authority, he is respected and his word is followed without question. He commands a position that will elevate him over the police, and rather than collaborate, he will dictate," Sylvia replied with a heavy sigh.

"Do you know that for certain, or is that just how you feel about the man?" the doctor asked, feeling rather offended on behalf of a man he had not met.

"Does it matter?" Sylvia asked. "Or do you question my judgement because I am merely a companion with a colourful history that makes me unsuitable for most normal society?"

"Peace, Sylvia, peace," Richard soothed. He knew that she was upset by the attack on her mistress, but he could also tell she was afraid for herself and what would happen if

Lady Sarah did not survive.

"No, I would hear the answer. Am I not entitled to an opinion of a man because his station in life is so far above mine?" Sylvia demanded and was met with a stony silence. "Very well, then by all means, investigate with Mr Arbuthnot."

She stood without waiting for a reply and stormed from the room. Lee and Stanley cast a glance between them, scowled at the doctor and Constable Evans and then chased after the retreating back of Lady Sarah's companion.

"That could have been handled better," Richard said, looking meaningfully at his father, before standing and following the other three.

The doctor shook his and watched the

four talking at the end of the hallway, as they were joined by Countess Szonja.

"Well, what a fine mess this all is. Come, we should go speak with Mr Arbuthnot and render our assistance. I am sure Mr Hunter shall do the same when he returns," Jack said firmly.

The brigadier sighed and slumped in his chair. The events of the evening had left him feeling quite drained and he desperately wanted time away from people to process his own grief at what had happened.

Arwyn was not sure what he should do, but as a policeman, he would have to follow whatever instruction the chief constable had handed down, at least for the moment. Though, he doubted very much that Sylvia was wrong.

Chapter 5

The chief constable was embroiled in a rather heated discussion with Mr Charles Arbuthnot when the doctor and constable re-entered the ballroom. Sylvia, Countess Szonja, Richard and the Baker boys were stood a short distance away talking to one another in hushed tones.

Mr Oliver Henry Brown was looking expectantly at the Chief Constable, wanting there to miraculously be some way of finding the responsible party and punishing them.

"Ah doctor, constable, come, come," Charles said as he noticed the two men entering the room. "We have come to terms and I will need you both at my side."

"I am sorry, Mr Arbuthnot, but I will have to return to the hospital in the morning. I can provide you with information, but my place is at Lady Sarah's side," Doctor Hales replied firmly. There was something in the tone of the former diplomat that rankled the doctor, and he was beginning to feel that perhaps Sylvia had not been overreacting at all.

"Of course, of course, how foolish of me, but dear Constable Evans, you will serve at my right hand, yes? Good!" Charles said without waiting for a response.

Captain Jonnes Smith cast an apologetic glance in Arwyn's direction, but it was so subtle that only the constable saw it, and even then he did not believe what he had seen. The chief constable was not known for his sympathy to the lower ranks, or those that did not know their place in society.

Mr Charles Arbuthnot not only knew his place, but often placed himself above those that had forged successful careers in certain fields. He was an extremely learned man, and had a good deal of experience in the field of diplomacy, but Sylvia doubted he had the abilities to investigate an attempted poisoning any more competently than Captain Jonnes Smith's men.

"My dear friend, thank you so much for your patience. I know that you are all keen to hear news of her ladyship, and the doctor will provide it in a moment. The chief constable and I have been in conference, and in order to facilitate an easy investigation, we ask that you would give your names and where you are staying in the area before you depart for the evening to Constables Cantello and McIntyre who are station at the far door. If you have business that means you will need to return home to other parts of the country without delay, then please come directly to myself or Constable Evans and we shall speak to you now," Mr Arbuthnot announced to the room, causing a rapt hush to fall upon the rather busy room.

"If there are any amongst your number that wish to remain to help with the investigation, we would be most grateful for you help," he finished and then waved for the doctor to take centre stage.

It did not take Jack long to inform the gathered crowd the grave nature of Lady Sarah's condition, and once he had delivered the news he left the ballroom for the safety of the brigadier's office.

Charles Arbuthnot expected the manor would soon empty and a small contingent of useful people would remain to help with finding Lady Sarah's assassins.

But very few people departed and half an hour after his announcement the ballroom was still filled with people.

The former diplomat sighed and shook his head before he began to make his way through the crowd looking for those that would be of use to him. Too many cooks would spoil his broth and he was determined to not be made to look foolish in front of the chief constable or the esteemed guests that had been in attendance.

Lord Arthur Montgomery Baird was sat to one side of the room, watching Charles with great interest. He did not find it even slightly amusing that his niece had been targeted by an assassin, and he felt that Mr Arbuthnot had overreached.

He watched as the former diplomat took several individuals to one side and spoke to them in a quiet voice. When there seven men gathered, he made a second announcement, thanking everyone for remaining but that they would best help the investigation by returning to their homes and lodgings.

There was a great deal of mumbling and

grumbling as the hall slowly emptied, Constable Cantello and Constable McIntyre stopping each of the guests to obtain their names and addresses.

Lord Arthur did not depart. He was staying at the manor, but he had not been approached, nor had he expected to be, but he wished to see what was about to happen.

Sylvia waited until the hall had emptied. The seven men that Mr Arbuthnot had chosen were the Duke of Wellington, Mr William Egerton MP, Mr Thomas Egerton, Mr Edward Egerton, Mr Claydon, Mr Christian, Constable Evans, Wilson, Richard Hales, and Mr Christopher, the verger.

Sylvia approached the former diplomat as he began to speak to the group of men with the

Baker boys and the countess flanking her.

"And what is it that you would have us do?" Sylvia asked in a rather sneering tone.

"Madam, your assistance, though I am sure is desperately important in many matters, is not required here," Mr Arbuthnot replied with practised politeness.

"You cannot think we have nothing to contribute," Sylvia countered.

"On the contrary, I think your contribution can be easily measured and would be best in the form of caring for your master," the former diplomat replied.

"I am not a slave or indentured servant. I do not have a master, I have an employer," Sylvia retorted, as she turned sharply on her heel and marched off, with the Baker boys and countess following close behind.

"And I suppose that you don't need the help of a colonial either?" Mr Brown asked with narrowed eyes.

"Sir, though I am sure you are much valued by your countrymen, there are certain ways things are done here in England, and I fear you will not understand them," Mr Arbuthnot replied with a shrug.

"Very well," Mr Brown said and followed after the retreating backs of his friends.

Lord Arthur smiled to himself and after a moment or two of listening to Charles Arbuthnot directing his troops, Lady Sarah's uncle quietly rose and followed after Sylvia.

Chapter 6

Charles Arbuthnot had some very particular ideas about how an investigation was to be run, and for Constable Evans, it was almost unbearable.

He appreciated that the former diplomat was worried and trying to do all that he could to help find those responsible, but it did not mean that there was not a right and wrong way for these things to be done.

It became very clear, early on, that his manner of talking to people he considered as his subordinates only very thinly masked the condescension he felt towards them. His experiences as a diplomat had given him skills to talk people into doing tasks, but the tasks he was assigning were not accomplishing very much.

At least as far as Arwyn could tell. No information or thought processes were being shared, and those that had been chosen to work for Charles Arbuthnot had not been selected for their mental abilities.

Frustrating as it was to be ordered to help in this investigation, there was little Arwyn could do to escape from it. The chief constable had given his order to the police constable, and there would be dire and far reaching consequences if Arwyn disobeyed him.

Richard Hales, on the other hand, was not subject to the same restrictions.

When morning had dawned, Charles had

insisted that his group of investigators be woken at first light by Mrs Bosworth, and one of the stable boys was sent to bring Constable Evans from the police house.

Constable Thompson Buckley had managed to avoid being assigned to the investigation, and when Arwyn had offered him the chance to work with the former diplomat instead of him, the constable had laughed and replied,

"Not for all the gold in the mines of King Midas. Besides, you were requested. The chief constable told me that I should not be offended to simply be required to police the village on this occasion. Mr Arbuthnot has a special relationship with you that is vital to solving this case."

Arwyn did not see the humour in such a statement, and his frustrations were further compounded when he discovered that Constable Buckley was helping Sylvia's investigation contingent.

Charles Arbuthnot had gathered his investigators before breakfast and given them their marching orders, which meant that the feast Cooky had been preparing went untasted by the men.

They were sent out to talk to all the guests that had been in attendance, most of which were not happy about being woken so early for questioning.

The doctor had returned to the hospital before the men had been summoned with Baron Christian von Stockmar accompanying him at the queen's behest; and Richard was sent after him to ask specific questions of his father, things that the trainee doctor was sure that he would have been able to ask the night before, if Mr Arbuthnot had thought ahead.

But the journey to the hospital gave him the opportunity to see Lady Sarah for himself.

Despite the doctor's fears, she had survived the night, and though there was still a great deal of damage to her body, some of the colour had begun to return to her skin. She was still unconscious, but for the moment, she was out of danger.

Mr Hunter had not slept a wink, but Pattinson and Captain Finlay had both managed a few hours. When Richard arrived, Doctor Hales answered the paltry questions his son had been sent to ask, and then suggested that Richard take Mr Hunter home with him.

"There is nothing good that will come from you losing sleeping at her bedside. Captain Finlay, the baron, and Pattinson are more than capable of guarding her. Go home, Alexander, take some rest," Jack ordered, and after around half an hour of being brow beaten by the doctor, Richard, and the captain, Mr Hunter Webb-Kneelingroach had begrudgingly agreed.

They had travelled back to Grangeback in silence, and once Richard had provided the answers that Charles Arbuthnot had been awaiting, he resigned from the investigation.

"What was that about?" Mr Hunter asked as Richard left the brigadier's study, which

Charles had turned into his own for the course of the investigation.

"Wasting time and resources, and declining the help of Sylvia, the Baker boys, and Countess Szonja," Richard shrugged.

"I assume that has not stopped them from investigating on their own?" Alex asked.

"We shall soon find out," Richard shrugged in reply. He had not seen Sylvia or had the chance to speak with her since Mr Arbuthnot had turned away her assistance the night before, but he, like Mr Hunter, assumed that the others would not let being excluded from the official investigation stop them from sleuthing.

The countess and Sylvia were in the conservatory with Mrs Claydon, all sipping tea.

The Baker boys were nowhere to be seen and both Richard and Alex found it extremely telling that they were absent.

"Ah gentlemen, so good to see you both, won't you join us? Mrs Claydon was just telling us about what she saw yesterday," the countess greeted them both with a broad smile.

"How fares her ladyship?" Sylvia asked immediately of Mr Hunter as the two men sat.

"She is improving, slowly. The doctor sent me home to rest, but I fear I will not rest until I know she will be safe," Mr Hunter replied with a shake of his head.

"Come, Mr Hunter, do not despair. All are striving to find her poisoner. She will be safe again soon," Mrs Claydon assured him. "Mr Brown and Constable Buckley have been set to work in the village, the Baker boys have gone to Chester, and the countess and Miss Lennox have been most studious in their work within the manor."

"And what has been discovered so far?" Mr Hunter asked.

"Very little, I am afraid. The guests were not watching for poisoners," Sylvia shrugged. "But our friends should report back shortly with news that will help us."

"Where is my father?" Mr Hunter asked.

"He is in his rooms. Bronwyn has taken charge of his care and well-being, and Edryd has taken on the duties of entertaining the dukes, duchess, princes and princesses who are all staying at the manor. Derwyn and Katherine, though I suppose you call her Annie, are keen to help however they can, but considering what happened in Wales, they have been designated as heralds," Sylvia replied.

"Heralds?" Richard frowned.

"Yes, we thought it sounded better than 'stay at the house and tell those that call any news they wish to hear'," Countess Szonja said with a slight smile.

"Yes, I feel heralds is a much better term," Richard agreed.

"Now, what should we know?"

The brigadier had managed to sleep some small amount, but requested that Mrs Bosworth bring him his breakfast in his room. He had no desire to quit the privacy of his chambers whilst his heart was broken.

He had lost much in his life. Men under his command, friends that had served beside him, his wife, his mistress, and his daughter. All he had left in the world had been his son, and his ward.

Now his ward teetered on the brink of death, and his son was faced with losing the woman he loved.

He often felt like he was cursed in many ways, but at the same time knew that this was, most likely, nothing to do with him. It was more likely that the enemies Lady Sarah had made in recent times were responsible, but that knowledge did not lessen the guilt.

Mrs Bosworth was run rather ragged by the guests in the house and she was not in any mood to take care of the brigadier in his melancholy when the rest of the household was having to keep going.

After she had brought his breakfast tray, she had been summoned to three different rooms to assist guests, and Bronwyn had watched her with a great deal of sympathy.

The Welsh farmer's wife waited until Mrs Bosworth emerged from the third room, looking rather frazzled, before she informed the housekeeper that she would be taking over the care of the brigadier from her, and that Edryd would take over as host.

Mrs Bosworth had been so shocked by Bronwyn's words that the stern and composed housekeeper broke down in floods of tears.

Bronwyn was not phased by this at all and with motherly affection, put her strong arms around Mrs Bosworth's shoulders, holding her tightly and consoling her until she managed to stem the flow of tears.

"Thank you, Mrs Evans," Mrs Bosworth said as she wiped her face on her apron.

"Bronwyn, and Edryd, none of this Mr and Mrs. Not at a time like this," Bronwyn insisted and Mrs Bosworth could not help but smile. "And tell Cooky, if she needs an afternoon off, you just tell me and I will stand in."

"You are very kind," Mrs Bosworth said appreciatively. "I should have expected as much, given the man that your son is."

"That is the nicest thing anyone has said to me in a long time," Bronwyn said, genuinely taken aback by the unexpected praise.

Chapter
7

The Foreign Office were a useful resource at time, but it wasn't something that anyone could call upon. That was one of the major advantages of Charles Arbuthnot's involvement in the investigation.

He may have lacked the inherent ability to investigate, but he had friends in high places who did possess the skill.

Mr Claydon and Mr Christian had proven to be very effective at questioning the guests from the wedding, though they had gleaned much of information about where everyone had been, they had been unsuccessful in finding any motive amongst the guests, and none of them had seen anything suspicious.

"Then if we cannot find the poisoner, we must find the poison," Mr Arbuthnot had decided after two days of fruitless questioning. He had not thought to speak with any of the staff at Grangeback, Duffleton Hall or Tatton Park, but the Egertons had spoken with those that worked for them and all had remarked that there had been three men they had never seen before in the kitchens.

Rather than tell Charles this information, they two younger Egertons had gone straight to Constable Evans, who, in turn had gone to Sylvia with the news.

The older Egertons had insisted on eventually telling Mr Arbuthnot, but he had dismissed the information.

"A kitchen with servants from different houses? Of course there would be those they did not know milling about."

But Sylvia was of a different opinion, and had asked Mr Brown to ask his staff if they had seen anything unusual.

Oliver Henry Brown wasted no time in returning to Duffleton Hall and summoning his staff.

"This may seem like a strange question for you, but the contingent from Tatton Park reported that there were three strangers in the kitchens at the manor when her ladyship was poisoned. Did any of you see the same?" he asked. He did not care that he was asking a leading question. Time was of the essence in his mind and the sooner the poisoner was found, the better.

"Sir," one of the footman said. "I didn't see three men. I saw four. They were dressed differently, and didn't seem like they had been in service before."

"That's right, the older chap and those three rude young 'uns," another of the footmen chimed in.

"They kept getting in the way, and seemed to be trying to take plates before they were ready. Then they disappeared," the cook said.

"The three of you, come with me. I want you to try and remember all that you can about these four whilst we travel. Then you are going to tell every possible detail to my friends," Mr Brown said with a strange expression on his face. It was one of relief but also of great concern.

"Who will get dinner ready, sir?" the butler asked in a rather flat tone.

"It's all done," the cook replied. "Young Nancy can see that it is served."

"Then we shall return later this evening. I will ensure that the three of them eat before we come home," Mr Brown assured the butler, who nodded to his master.

The journey to Grangeback was passed in silence as the three members of Mr Brown's household thought long and hard about what they seen of the four men that night.

When they arrived, another carriage had pulled up, and a gentleman was disembarking from it.

"Good evening, sir, can I help?" Mr Brown called out of his carriage window.

"I have been asked to call, sir. Wait, I know you. Mr Brown is it not?" the man said as he turned round.

"Mr Harry Taylor, this is a surprise. You have arrived to help, I suppose?" Mr Brown said as he opened the door and leapt out of the carriage.

"My employer was quite insistent," Mr Taylor replied with a grin. "And I am only too happy to oblige."

"Then come, you have arrived at quite the right moment. We have some news to share," Mr Brown said as his employees stepped out of his carriage, and the five of them made their way into the manor.

Chapter 8

Of all the investigations that the Baker boys had been involved in, the case of Lady Sarah's poisoner was one that Lee and Stanley would not forget. They were both worried about their mentor, not for their own sakes, but because the future of such a generous woman was now in question.

They had felt quite spurned when Mr Arbuthnot had said their help was not needed, but glad that Sylvia had insisted on investigating, regardless of his instructions.

They knew that a great deal of faith had been placed in their abilities when they had been dispatched to Chester. They had not ridden on their own in one of the brigadier's carriages before, and normally this kind of event would have been viewed with a great deal of excitement.

But with their thoughts focused on the task before them, the Baker boys usual boundless energy and joy was somewhat muted.

"She won't die, will she?" Lee asked suddenly, breaking the silence that the two boys had been travelling in.

"No, she can't," Stanley replied far more firmly than he had expected. He barely believed his own words as they were based more on hope than fact.

"Right," Lee said. The conviction in his brother's voice was enough to settle his own nerves, even if he only chose to believe Stanley because that is what he wanted to hear.

They lapsed back into silence for the rest of their journey to Chester and focused on the job that lay before them.

When the carriage lurched to a halt, they were outside one of the more reputable chemists that they city had to offer. Mr Charnley was an old friend of Doctor Hales and extremely well thought of in his profession. He had many linctures, tinctures and tonics that were very effective, as well as medicines, poisons and other chemicals that caused Lee and Stanley to be transfixed with wonder the moment they stepped through the door.

The shop was laid out around a long horseshoe counter that ran from one side of the door to the other. It was made from dark mahogany that seemed to suck in all light from around it, and though the gas lamps burned brightly, the place seemed by dark.

Great shelves of mahogany towered behind the counter and reached up to the ceiling, filled with glass jars and other wonders.

"Good morning, can I help you sirs?" Mr Charnley asked from behind the counter. He was a well presented man with extremely tidy hair and very well manicured nails. He was as fastidious in how neatly his shop was kept as well as his appearance.

"We've come from Grangeback Manor," Lee began. He was aware that they were often overlooked because of their appearance as young and wiry boys that often forgot how important washing their hands and face were.

"Ah, bad business," Mr Charnley said darkly.

"Indeed. I am surprised you know of it," Stanley said slowly.

"The city is alive with talk of nothing else," Mr Charnley replied. "It is tragic for such a young bride to be struck down at her engagement feast. She will be missed."

"She isn't dead," Lee said defensively.

"My apologies, young sir, I had heard she died. I am glad to hear the gossip is wrong," Mr Charnley replied. "What of this tragic matter can I assist you with?"

"We are interested in poisons," Stanley replied. "Our lady was poisoned and we must find out who is responsible."

"Ah, I see. Well, I have my poisons record here. Let me see. When do you wish to look at?" Mr Charnley asked.

"The last five days before the engagement ball," Lee replied darkly, still not having forgiven the chemist for assuming Lady Sarah had died.

"Do you wish all the names?" Mr Charnley asked.

"No, not all the names. You can discount people you have sold to before or regularly I should say," Stanley said.

"Ah, so new customers or those who only purchase seldom items?" Mr Charnley said.

"Yes, that will be fine," Lee agreed with his brother.

"Then, young sirs, you are in luck, only

one man, as he was certainly no gentleman, has purchased rat poison from me four days ago. I have his address here. I thought it unusual as he had come clear across the city, and there are at least four other chemists between his abode and this humble shop," Mr Charnley said as he took a small piece of paper from under the counter and began to write the name and address of the man upon it.

"Thank you," Stanley said as he took the paper from the chemist.

"You are most welcome. Please, do give my regards to her ladyship, and wish her a speedy recovery," Mr Charnley said as he watched the two boys turn and leave the shop.

"Is that him do you think?" Lee asked as he looked at the paper in his brother's hand.

"Maybe, but Sylvia said to visit all the chemists and ask the same question. We can't just assume we've found him straight away. People do get rats," Stanley replied with a sigh.

The brothers spent the day going from one chemist to another until they had visited every one of them. Lee had become increasingly irritable as every chemist had heard the same rumour as Mr Charnley, that Lady Sarah was dead, and he was tired of having to tell people she was still alive.

The more he had to correct gossip, the less he began to believe that her ladyship was still alive, and Stanley began to talk more and more so that Lee could seethe without preventing them gathering the information they needed.

It was late in the evening when they finally returned to Grangeback, armed with the names of nine people that had all purchased arsenic, cyanide, and strychnine in a similar time frame and were not regular customers of the chemists.

When they arrived at the manor, Mr Taylor was already there, and Mr Brown's staff had passed on their information and were in the kitchens, enjoying a well earned supper prepared by Cooky.

"This man here, he said he bought rat poison, but he asked for cyanide," Richard frowned as he looked at the piece of paper that Mr Charnley had given the boys.

"Why is that strange?" Mr Brown asked.

"Because arsenic and strychnine are much

more effective for killing rats," Mr Hunter said. "Cyanide can be used, but why would you if you can get the other two."

"Indeed. Besides, Lady Sarah's symptoms are much more common to cyanide poisoning," Richard said thoughtfully.

"Then you believe we should start with this man?" Sylvia asked.

"Yes. It is a wonder she survived this, truly," Richard said with amazement. "It is a truly deadly poison."

"Then let us be grateful that she did, or that the poisoners were inept," Constable Buckley replied.

"Yes, I wonder if it was the food she had eaten that caused the effects to be limited," Richard began.

"There is no time for such ponderances now," Sylvia snapped.

"No indeed. I think that Mr Taylor, Mr Hunter, and Mr Hales should try to steal Constable Evans and investigate how she was poisoned. Was it food, drink, injection, a gas, speak to Mrs Bosworth and Cooky now we know there were four of them," Countess Szonja said firmly.

"Mr Brown, Lee, Stanley, Constable Buckley and I will visit the names of these pieces of paper and try to find some answers there," Sylvia said.

"Good. I shall remain here and see what I can learn of what information our rival investigation has discovered, and wait for any news from the hospital of course," the countess smiled.

"We shall begin in the morning then," Mr Hunter agreed and the party all went to their beds feeling somewhat exhausted but that they were at least making progress.

Chapter 9

Lady Sarah opened her eyes and felt the sting of the hospital lamps almost instantly. Her lungs burned and her limbs felt heavy. She was uncertain of where she was or why she came to be there, but for a moment, panic gripped her chest.

The last thing she remembered was sitting at the table during her engagement feast. Now she was in unfamiliar surroundings. She opened her mouth to call out for help, but a sudden bark stopped her. It was a familiar sound and one that told her she was in no immediate danger.

"Pattinson," she croaked and felt the

Akita lick her hand in response before rubbing his head up against it.

"My lady, you are awake," another familiar sound reached her ears.

"Captain Finlay?" she asked and slowly turned her head to look at where the captain sat.

"Indeed, and the Baron von Stockmar is here as well," the captain replied with a look of relief on his face.

"I will fetch the doctor," Christian said and disappeared from the room.

"Where am I?" Lady Sarah asked as she tried to sit up and failed.

"The hospital, in Manchester. You were poisoned and it was not known whether you were going to survive the first night, let alone wake. Though, I suppose that we should all have had a little more faith in you," Captain Finlay said with mild amusement.

"Indeed," Lady Sarah replied. "But poisoned? Why?"

"That is a question that many are seeking to answer as we speak. You are cut from a rather unique cloth, and being such means that you inspire people to either great loyalty or to great hatred," the captain mused. "So I must ask, can you think of anyone that might hate you enough to try and kill you in such a public way?"

"There are many at court who resent my standing with the queen, my own relatives included. It is possible that I am facing some repercussions from the incident with the slave traders we encountered in Brighton, and of course, there is Fitzwilliam," Lady Sarah said with a slight shake of her head. "Is that enough?"

"I should think so, at least for now," another voice answered from the doorway on the opposite side of the room.

"Uncle!" Lady Sarah said with all the delight she could muster as she turned her head to face the newcomer.

Lord Arthur Montgomery Baird was stood in the doorway, leaning on his cane with Doctor Hales and Baron von Stockmar flanking him.

"I came to see how you fared, and I am very gratified that you chose to awaken for my visit," his lordship replied with a grin.

"I do not think we should keep you awake too long, your ladyship. You have endured a great deal and sleep will be the best aid to your recovery," the doctor said firmly as the three made their way into the room.

"Allow me five minutes with my niece, and then I shall return to the manor. I am sure that they will all wish to know how she fares," Lord Arthur argued.

"Very well, five minutes, but no more. Then I shall have to ask you to leave. The captain and baron will be here with Pattinson to watch over her," the doctor replied.

"Where is Mr Hunter?" Lady Sarah asked. She had wanted to ask the question from the moment she opened her eyes but had feared knowing the answer.

"He is at Grangeback. He refused to leave your side or take any rest, so I sent him home. He would be no good making himself ill. It would not make you any better," the doctor replied.

"Then, uncle, will you tell him I am sorry to worry him so?" Lady Sarah asked.

"I will, but I feel he will find it a most foolish apology," Lord Arthur replied as he sat beside his niece in what was Baron von Stockmar's chair.

"We shall wait outside," Captain Finlay said and left the lord and lady alone to talk with Pattinson close at their side.

"With enemies of that range, it would be advisable for all those investigating to work together," Baron von Stockmar said as the captain closed the door to the room.

"Are they not?" Captain Finlay asked.

"No, Mr Arbuthnot chose a certain few to investigate and almost none of them were part of Lady Sarah's inner circle," the doctor replied.

"Indeed? That seems somewhat short-sighted," Captain Finlay said with surprise.

"Perhaps, but if her ladyship is right that it is one of those parties that are responsible, then the skills of her friends and the influence of Mr Arbuthnot will both be needed," the baron replied.

"I will inform his lordship when they are finished. He will be more than happy to bring them all into line, I would imagine," the doctor said.

"How so?" Christian frowned.

"His lordship is quite taken with Sylvia. He will enjoy informing Mr Arbuthnot of her value and his own folly," the doctor replied with a slight chuckle.

"I think there are many others would be happy to do such, if only to point out his folly," the baron smiled.

"Pride makes fools of us all," Captain Finlay said almost automatically as he was thinking on something that was bothering him. "If you will excuse me for a moment. I must send a letter."

Chapter 10

The following morning, breakfast was a bright affair. Lord Arthur had returned with good news and the brigadier had finally emerged from his chambers. The royals in residence were all filled with a joy that her ladyship was awake, and made plans to visit later that day.

The brigadier had a great deal of correspondence to attend to with the news that Lady Sarah was awake, so he did not delay, and after breakfast, went to evict Mr Arbuthnot from his study.

The library was being used by Sylvia and the countess for their investigation, which meant that Mr Arbuthnot was forced to consider the billiards room, until Lord Arthur requested an audience with both the countess and the former diplomat.

The Duke of Wellington had joined the group, who made their way to the library to talk. He did not say a word, and so far had done little to nothing to help with the investigation. He did not see the use in splitting their forces, and had told Charles on no less than three occasions that he was being foolish.

So when Lord Arthur told them of the enemies that were potentially targeting Lady Sarah, and their need to work as one team rather than two separate entities, the duke felt quite vindicated, though he had the good grace to not be so crass to tell Mr Arbuthnot 'I told you so.'

It was enough to hear him reprimanded by Lady Sarah's uncle, and be told he would need to apologise to Sylvia at the earliest opportunity.

Rather than stay and listen to the countess and former diplomat trading information, the duke decided to join the group on their visit to the hospital to see Lady Sarah, and the royals were only too happy to have him along.

Though he had not always been the most popular figure in court, he was a hero to the people, and there was no doubt that some press would be searching to publish the royal angle of this poisoning saga.

To see a hero with the royals visiting her ladyship, a now well-known pillar of justice, could only help to solidify public opinion.

Their carriages lurched away not long after Sylvia, Mr Brown, Constable Buckley, Lee and Stanley had departed.

Harry stood watch from the drawing window, and the moment they left, he signalled to Arwyn, Richard and Alex that now was the time to find Mrs Bosworth.

Derwyn had taken Miss DeVille for a walk in the gardens as the day was surprisingly bright and warm for the time of year, and Edryd and Bronwyn were enjoying a quite respite together in the conservatory.

It was the quietest the manor house had been in weeks and was the perfect opportunity to speak with Mrs Bosworth without earning her ire.

"What can I do for you gentlemen?" Mrs Bosworth asked rather wearily when the four young men cornered her in the smaller dining room.

"There were four men that served food and drink on the night of the ball. The staff of both Duffleton Hall and Tatton Park had never seen them before," Mr Hunter began.

"Oh yes, the four men from Chester. What of them?" Mrs Bosworth asked.

"You know of them?" Richard frowned.

"Well of course I do. I would be a poor housekeeper had I not checked who was coming into the kitchen," Mrs Bosworth said rather dryly.

"Aside from Chester, where did they come from?" Mr Taylor asked.

"They gave me a card. Said the brigadier had engaged them to help," Mrs Bosworth said thoughtfully before she reached into her apron and pulled out a rather crumpled looking rectangular piece of white card.

"Did you question the brigadier about it?" Mr Hunter asked with a look of alarm.

"Of course not. I am not in the business of questioning my employers decision," Mrs Bosworth snorted.

"You did not think it strange that only four men would be engaged and that no mention of it was made before hand?" Mr Taylor asked rather pointedly.

Mrs Bosworth stopped dead in her tracks and turned slowly to look at the four men before her.

"They are behind this?" she asked, her hands shaking.

Richard moved quickly and pulled out a chair and guided Mrs Bosworth into it before she collapsed. Mr Hunter closed his eyes and held the bridge of his nose with two fingers as he fought the urge to chastise her.

"Do you remember what you asked them to do?" Mr Taylor asked gently.

"Two of them where to help Cooky, the other two were to serve the food," Mrs Bosworth said rather helplessly.

"Then it was in her food. The two who helped Cooky put it on a specific dish and the other two ensured she was served it," Richard sighed.

"What did they use?" Mrs Bosworth

asked.

"Cyanide, we think," Constable Evans said and nodded to Harry to take Mr Hunter from the room. "We need you to think now. Do you remember anything they talked about, anything we can use to find them?"

"I, I don't know. I just have the card," Mrs Bosworth stammered.

"I'll fetch Bosworth and Cooky," Richard said and left Mrs Bosworth in Constable Evans' care for the moment. Out in the hallway, Mr Hunter was pacing back and forth with frustration.

"You will have to forgive her at some point." Harry said rather pointedly, but Mr Hunter shot him a dark look.

"If she had only asked my father, they

would never have gained access to the house,"
Mr Hunter spat.

"Indeed, they would have, slipped in with all the guests from the village, or with visiting dignitaries. They would have found a way no matter what Mrs Bosworth did. It is not her fault any more than it is your fault, and you need to keep a level head on your shoulders. We haven't found them yet and we only have a white rectangle of card to help us," Harry warned him.

Mr Hunter took a deep breath and huffed.

"Fine. I will go tell her she is forgiven and it is not her fault," Mr Hunter said with a sever lack of grace.

"Try to sound at least a little sincere, will you?" Harry said as Mr Hunter stomped back towards the small dining room. He froze and looked at Harry, who gave him a rather pointed stare in return.

"Why did Lady de Mandeville send you again?" Mr Hunter asked, a small amount of good humour creeping into his voice.

"Because you needed me," Harry shrugged.

"I don't know if I said it last time, but I am glad she didn't kill you," Mr Hunter replied.

Harry laughed and leant against the wall to keep himself from doubling over.

"I am too, though it would have been no thanks to you!" he shot back, and Mr Hunter entered the small dining room with a smile on his face.

Chapter 11

The carriage lurched forwards into one of the less desirable areas of Chester. Stanley and Lee stared out of the windows at the people they passed and Sylvia shifted uncomfortably in her seat.

"What is it?" Mr Brown asked, seeing her discomfort.

"The last time I was in this area, I was begging. It is not a pleasant memory," Sylvia admitted.

"You were a beggar?" Constable Buckley asked with surprise.

"I was cast out into the street and saved from it by her ladyship, that is all you need to know," Sylvia said rather testily and the two men dropped the topic.

The carriage stopped at the address they had been given and the Baker boys were the first to leap out. They ran over to the windows, and rudely, peered inside.

"He's on the floor, not moving," Lee called back to the three adults that were alighting from the carriage.

"Is he dead?" Constable Buckley asked.

"Hard to tell from here, but probably," Stanley replied.

"Why probably?" Constable Buckley replied.

"We are always finding men like him dead. They do the dirty deed for some else and end up dead to keep them quiet," Sylvia replied.

"Then why would any one work for those hiring them?" Constable Buckley asked in confusion.

"Desperation mostly, other times greed. It's hard to feel pity for the greedy ones. The desperate ones you often find yourself feeling for them," Mr Brown shrugged.

Constable Buckley looked astounded at how jaded his four companions sounded, but did not press the matter as he followed them around to the door of the rooms the man had taken.

The door was open, and it was clear that he had been dead for a few days from the smell that dominated the room.

"I will have to send for the coroner,"

Constable Buckley said as he stepped away from the room to keep himself from vomiting.

"We'll take you in the carriage," Lee volunteered.

"Then we can go back and tell the others he is dead," Stanley agreed.

"Is it me, or does he look familiar to you?" Sylvia asked Mr Brown as the Baker boys and constable disappeared.

"Now that you mention it, he does. Where do you know him from?" Mr Brown asked.

"He was at the ball, but I am sure that he was following me a few days before. I was fetching certain supplies for the ball. Cooky also mentioned that she felt someone was watching her when she came into Chester on her day off a few weeks ago. I wonder if he has been watching us for that long," Sylvia said as she bit her lip in thought.

"It is entirely possible he was, and if he was one of the men at the ball-" Mr Brown began.

"He was," Sylvia said with certainty.

"-then the other three were probably watching you and others from Grangeback as well," Mr Brown finished.

"We should look around and see if we can find any clues as to who the other men are and might be found," Sylvia said.

"Do you think he would keep such things?" Oliver asked with a slightly raised eyebrow.

"If it were me and I was involved with a

deadly business, I would have names, addresses and whatever else I could gather on those I was working for and with, as insurance that I would survive the affair," Sylvia replied.

"Perhaps he was not that sensible, he is dead after all," Mr Brown shrugged.

"He is, but we should look anyway," Sylvia replied and began to search through the dead man's belongings.

Chapter 12

Derwyn was glad to see Miss DeVille looking so happy and strong. The air of Stickleback Hollow had certainly been agreeing with her, and the news that Lady Sarah would survive her poisoning had brightened all spirits around the house and village.

The unexpectedly warm and bright day had been equally welcomed and they decided to take a tour of the greenhouse where Lady Sarah had cultivated a great number of roses that bloomed all year round. The gardener had worried that they would exhaust themselves, but the warm temperature, the fresh fertiliser from the stables and a great deal of care meant that they had continued to be in steady health.

It was a rather pleasant and fragrant place to pass time, and there were several beautiful benches that were placed around the great structure of glass and metal, which allowed Katherine DeVille to sit and rest when necessary.

There was a great breeze that was allowed through the greenhouse as well, there were great glass panels that the head gardener opened to allow the movement of air, but limit how much cold and rain could infiltrate.

It was closing on lunch time when Edryd and Bronwyn came down from the house to join them, as they entered the greenhouse, some small movement at the corner of his vision caught Derwyn's eye.

He turned sharply and saw a man snooping around in the floor beds close to the manor. Derwyn did not wait, nor did he greet his parents, but set of at a run.

The moment he was free of the greenhouse, he roared at the intruder,

"Hey! What do you think you are doing? Get out of here!"

Derwyn had no reason to fear such a skulking shadow, but as he drew nearer to him, he realised the intruder was not alone, and was suddenly faced with an assault of three men all armed with wooden clubs.

Edryd had noticed the man the moment Derwyn had set off running. Leaving Bronwyn to look after Annie, he followed his son, and what had been a rather one-sided ambush was now a much more even affair.

The sound of Derwyn yelling was also heard by Mr Christian and Mr Claydon who were returning from speaking with some of the guests who were billeted at Wilson's inn.

Hearing the commotion, they advanced, and the numbers advantage was gone. Sensing that more men would soon appear from the house, the three men dropped their weapons and fled the scene.

Countess Szonja watched the events unfolding from the window in the library and decided at once to send for the local militia. The colonel's wife was a good friend of the countess and she knew they would come and her urging.

"What reason could they have for attacking here?" Lord Arthur asked, as the countess scribbled a hasty note to her friend.

"Perhaps they have heard that Lady Sarah survived her attempted assassination and have come to finish their assignment," the countess replied absently, and then realised what she had said. "The hospital, we must warn them."

"No message we can send will reach them in time, I fear. But do not fret, there are friends there now who are more than a match for brutes such as these," Lord Arthur said kindly.

Captain Finlay was dozing in his chair when the sound of the door being opened roused him. The visit from the royals and duke had been rather exhausting for everyone save for the baron.

Christian had elected to walk the party back to their carriages, and left Captain Finlay and Pattinson to watch over Lady Sarah in his absence.

"Back so soon?" the captain said quiet groggily, but soon realised his mistake. Instead of Baron Christian von Stockmar standing in the room, a man dressed in filthy clothing was stood there instead.

He was a broad shouldered man with menace in his eyes, but he was surprised to find that her ladyship was not alone in the room.

Pattinson was on his feet and growling in a moment, and Captain Finlay leapt from his chair and reached for his walking stick that was leaning against the wall.

"You think a dog and a stick will beat me?" the man in the doorway sneered.

"That depends on whether you have considered that this is not a stick, it is a sword," Captain Finlay said as he drew his blade and stood ready for the man.

"Stick or sword, makes no difference. Men like you are cowards, fed and fattened, too soft to fight real men," the stranger continued to sneer.

"I see, then perhaps I will be able to better your opinion of men such as I, and I am sure Pattinson will change your mind as to your low opinion of dogs," the captain said.

Pattinson barked twice and stayed by his

mistress' side. The dog knew that he was the last line of defence, should the captain fall, and he would give his last breath to prevent harm coming to his mistress.

The man advanced into the room and swung, aiming to knock Captain Finlay off his feet before he could use his blade, but the captain had expected such an action and with a mere flick of his wrist, he managed to slice the wrist of the man, causing him to falter and retreat.

"You bastard," the man swore.

"Come now, there is no need for such language in front of a lady," the captain smiled and advanced. The onslaught with the fine blade was brutal, and rather unexpected. Captain Finlay had not grown up a man from wealth and privilege, but rather was a man that had come from rather humble beginnings, and he had seen many men like this thug before. He knew the type of man he was facing.

He had also honed his skills over many years. He had poured his blood, sweat and tears into becoming the finest swordsman in the land of not only England but India as well. There was no man that had heard his name who believed that he could be beaten when he held a blade in his hand.

It took eight precise and painful slashes from the sword to convince the brute that his mission was doomed to failure, and that he should flee before he lost more than blood.

The moment he turned to flee, Pattinson knew that it was his turn to act. He had been in this position many times before, and launched his attack. His giant and sharp teeth sank into the man's posterior, causing him to yell out in pain.

The dog was determined to leave his mark and a last memory of why no man should try to harm any he guarded.

The yell attracted the attention of not only the doctors and nurses in the hospital, but the baron, who was returning.

As soon as the baron and Doctor Hales had seized hold of the man and Captain Finlay had placed his blade against the man's neck Pattinson released his quarry.

A policeman had been sent for and it was Constable McGill that answered the call. It did not take but a moment for the attempt on Lady

Sarah's life to be relayed to the constable and the thug was cuffed and led away.

"I think that it might be best if we were to return home," the baron said as he looked at the sleeping lady.

"I will speak to my colleagues, but you may be right. She can be far better protected at Grangeback than here and there is only so much more that our medicines can do for her. Rest and care will serve far better now she is gaining back her strength," the doctor agreed.

Chapter
18

The doctors all agreed that Lady Sarah would be much better at Grangeback, rather than remaining at the hospital.

It had taken a day for all the necessary preparations to be made before she was transported back in a carriage. Mr Hunter abandoned the investigation to be there to travel with Lady Sarah back to Grangeback, and she was very glad to see him.

The colonel of the militia had received the countess' request and had come at once to Grangeback. The brigadier had no objection to the sudden arrival of armed soldiers on his land, and Wilson was extremely glad of the extra custom, as the wives of some of the officers were billeted at his inn.

The colonel was mortified when he discovered the Duke of Wellington was at the manor, as well as a number of the royal family, and had insisted on parading his men properly for those gathered.

By the time Lady Sarah, Captain Finlay, Mr Hunter, Baron von Stockmar, Doctor Hales, and Pattinson arrived at Grangeback, the gardens around the manor were covered with tents and men were standing guard at different posts.

"Does this not seem excessive?" Lady Sarah asked wryly as she saw all the soldiers.

"Perhaps to you, but to those of us that have seen those men that have tried to kill you, it does not seem so," Mr Hunter replied gently.

Lady Sarah was escorted to her room and Mr Hunter took up guard with Captain Finlay and Pattinson.

The baron was glad to be relieved of guard duty, and had his own duties to take care of. Her friends were all there to welcome her home, and the princesses had all been keen to see her.

Once she was safely in her room and Cooky had begun creating a feast for, Sylvia, Mr Brown, Arwyn, Richard, Harry, Constable Buckley, and the Baker boys all met with the countess and Mr Arbuthnot in the library.

"We have had a letter from the coroner about the dead man you found," the countess began. "It seems he died from cyanide poisoning,."

"I doubt he appreciated the irony of it," Richard said dryly.

"No indeed, but we also have a name for the gentleman. He is a criminal of some small renown. He was one of Major Tyler's men," Mr Arbuthnot said.

"Who was Major Tyler?" Constable Buckley asked with a frown.

"He was one of Wellington's exploration officers - a spymaster if truth be told. Many of those that worked for him end up in the foreign office, but there are many who do not. Instead they become mercenaries, assassins, very expensive because they have been trained by the best that the army has to offer," the former diplomat explained.

"So an expensive mercenary, turned assassin who worked for one of the Duke of Wellington's officers is behind this?" Lee asked.

"If only it were that simple. He will be one of many, a cog in a greater machine, and sadly it is a machine that can afford to lose many parts," Charles Arbuthnot sighed.

"What about this company that Mrs Bosworth had the card from? What of them?" Harry asked. When Lord Arthur had ordered the two investigation teams to work together, the countess had thought it best that Mr Arbuthnot's contacts investigate the company that had supposedly sent the four men to the house.

"It does not exist. In fact, it is one of many ruses that men in this line of employment use in order to infiltrate their chosen targets and avoid detection," Mr Arbuthnot replied.

"Then what is there that we can do? These men have left no trail for us to follow, we do not know who has employed them, what is there that is left?" Richard asked with frustration.

"There is patience. Men like this do not stop. When they fail, they end up dead. When they succeed, they are rewarded. I do not doubt that the man you found dead was killed because Lady Sarah survived the attempt. He was the one who purchased the poison and did not succeed in his assassination so he was tied up, as they say," Mr Arbuthnot said.

"Then we simply sit in the house and do nothing?" Arwyn asked with a heavy sigh.

"Not at all, we have the militia here, thanks to the countess, and we have one of the greatest generals of our age here. We plan, my friends," Mr Arbuthnot said with a malicious grin.

"A warm welcome for those so keen to visit us," Sylvia said with equal venom.

"Yes, and as they chose to show no mercy, none shall be given in return," Mr Arbuthnot replied.

Chapter 14

Contrary to the belief in Stickleback Hollow, the brigadier was not a man who wished to take up the reins of command again. He had been happy to retire, and with the militia encamped on his land, many ad assumed he would start to issue orders to the the colonel, but he was far more concerned with his ward's safety.

It was the Duke of Wellington to whom the colonel had handed over command of his men, and the excitement in the camp had been palpable. There was nothing short of electricity running through the men at the prospect of being commanded by such a figure, a one who was a hero to so many.

The plan to protect Grangeback Manor was a simple one, the militia's camp would be broken and all their equipment would be stored in the ballroom with the curtains drawn.

The militia would make a great show of departing from the manor and parading through the village, only to return to the house via a secret passage that Lee and Stanley Baker had discovered during their time there.

It seemed to be an old escape for priests that ran a great distance across the lands and ended in the trees that still surrounded the village.

A handful of the men would be stationed under the direct command of the duke, whilst the others were split into two halves, one under the command of Captain Finlay, and the other under the command of their colonel.

These men would hide in the forests, shown paths to move about unseen by Mr Hunter, and would advance on the house once the alarm was raised, thereby cornering the remaining men and cutting the head from the snake.

The constables and Richard Hales would take up position on the Edge, a large outcropping of land that rose towards the sky behind the village, and watching any that might have escaped the trap and use those forces the constabulary in Chester could spare to ensure they did not leave the area.

The guests at the manor had all been removed and taken to the relative safety of

Wilson's inn, where they could wait out the conflict without fear of incurring any injury.

Lady Sarah could not be moved, not only for fear that she would be spotted by anyone watching the house, but that it would have a detrimental effect on her health to be moved so soon after she had arrived home.

The doctor had taken up his post by Lady Sarah's bedside with both Mr Hunter and Pattinson there to guard them both.

Bronwyn and Miss DeVille had also gone to Wilson's Mill to stay out of the path of the fighting, but Edryd and Derwyn had refused to leave, and along with those that remained from the investigators, they where assigned as lookouts from upper windows of the house, all save for the countess, who was now at Wilson's inn, Sylvia, and the Baker boys.

The latter three were told to go hide with the servants and to stay out of the path of the fighting. But none of the trio were strangers to violence.

Things were somewhat complicated by the arrival of Charles and Charlotte Egerton at the manor, who had come to enquire after the progress of the investigation on their mother's behalf.

The duke deemed it too great a risk to send the children back, in case they were captured and tortured for information, and they were sent to hide with Sylvia and the Baker boys.

What the duke did not realise is that there were a multitude of secret passages around the manor and that when he told the Baker boys to hide, to them it meant slip into the walls, ready to ambush unsuspecting invaders.

Something that Sylvia, Charlotte, and Charles Egerton, were only too happy to do as well.

Chapter 15

Almost three hours passed from the time the militia left in a blaze of fanfare to when they were all able to manoeuvre into position.

Though those in the house had no idea where those outside the house were, the men entering through the long secret passage had the furthest distance to travel, and therefore once they were in place, the assumption was made that everyone was ready.

Watches were set so that men could rest as the duke did not expect the assault to come in daylight. It gave the men time to rest and eat so that they would be fresh when the assault began.

At midnight, the duke ensured all his men were awake and ready to fight. Even if they had to wait for several hours, it was better than being caught unaware.

In the walls, Sylvia was developing a severe case of cramp and wanted to leap out and stretch, but she knew that it was better to endure the pain and ease it how she could rather than risk discovery.

At 2am the men on watch signalled movement outside the house and the word was passed for the men stationed inside to be ready.

Muskets were loaded and held ready, the discipline of trained troops on the verge of battle was a sight to behold, but in the darkness of Grangeback, the duke could only sense his men.

The door of the house was tested and pushed open, the large creaking piece of wood hiding the waiting forces. The moment it was open and the first man moved, guns cracked and the hallway was filled with acrid smoke from musket fire.

The sounds of musket balls striking wood, glass and the screams of them tearing into men's body filled the night, followed by glass shattering in other quarters of the house. More gunfire followed. The men needed no word from Wellington to fire at the intruders, they knew their duty and they had been well-trained.

The duke made a note somewhere in the back of his mind to congratulate the colonel. The sound of gunfire and fighting in the house was the cue for the forces to come streaming from the woods, and in mere moments a flood of red jackets had encircled the manor.

There would be no escaping.

Richard, Arwyn and Thompson watched the fray, or what they could discern of it from their vantage point using a spyglass that had been loaned to them by the duke.

Lamps were turned up after the first volley of fire and sheer numbers of mercenaries they faced became clear. There were twice as many as the duke had expected and with light, they could see their quarries.

They had studied the house and had come in at specifically chosen points. They did not seem to care if they died, only that they accomplished their mission.

But neither the militia nor the mercenaries had bet on the Baker boys. Lee and Stanley leapt from the walls and saved two of the militia from certain death. Sylvia was equally deadly, and just as unexpected, as were Charles and Charlotte.

Then the reinforcements came.

From the servant's quarters, the men and women who worked at the manor and called it home came streaming. Their fury unleashed, armed with kitchen knives, pots and pans, they were defending not only their home but their mistress.

A girl that had come to them as an orphan in need of a home, and had found one with them. There is an old saying that a man defending his home is far more deadly than a man who merely fights for money.

The truth of that was clearly shown in how the people of Grangeback fought for the manor and Lady Sarah.

"What is going on?" Richard asked from atop the Edge.

Down in the village, torches had been lit and people were coming out of all the buildings and heading towards the manor en masse, even those that had been moved to the inn for safety were with them.

"I think the mercenaries are getting more than the bargained for," Arwyn replied with a grin. His chest was filled with pride as he watched the townsfolk advancing.

"Shall we sweep for spies then?" Thompson asked and the other two agreed. A torch was lit and waved and the constables and sergeants of Cheshire began to make their way through the trees looking for any who might be hiding, watching the manor.

The three on the Edge descended, checking not only the old mine but the path on the way down to the forest below.

Panic had seized the mercenaries in the manor. It was fighting unlike any they had seen before and when they tried to turn and flee they were faced with the full fury of the militia and villagers who were waiting outside.

When the smoke had cleared, there were three of the militia dead, but twenty of the mercenaries and another twelve that were safely placed into the custody of the Cheshire police.

Charles Arbuthnot had been waiting for the battle to end and went with the policemen and their prisoners back to Chester so that he might assist with their questioning.

The damage to the manor was quite extensive, and there was a great deal of mess to clear up and set right, but what was most important was that the manor was safe, and so was Lady Sarah.

Chapter 16

Getting men to talk who did not wish to part with the information they safeguarded was a skill in which many of Charles Arbuthnot's friends excelled, and some of them had been only too happy to travel to Chester to put their skills to good use.

It is said that on the third day, everybody talks. It took less than one for the mercenaries to all be broken, and the information they had to share was interesting to say the least.

They had been hired by a man known only as the general, but he was not a hard man to locate from the description that was given. He was found trying to board a boat to

America, but it was not the police, the military or the men of the foreign office that found him.

Lady de Mandeville had many in her employ in both high and low places, and when she sought something, she was almost never denied it.

Her agents found the general and had him bound, gagged and on a ship sailing for India before the man knew what was happening to him. He would be received by her agents in India and given the punishment that the countess felt was fitting.

Captain Finlay and Mr Taylor had departed from Grangeback the morning after the assault and return to London, where Lady de Mandeville was waiting.

"Do they know yet that it was Fitzwilliam

behind this?" she asked as the two men sat in comfortable chairs sipping on the finest whisky that either of them had tasted in some time.

"Not yet. I am sure that Mr Arbuthnot shall inform them of it sooner rather than later. The search for the general continues, and until he is found, I suppose they shall keep it a mystery. Though, knowing her ladyship, she will discover the truth for herself sooner rather than later," Captain Finlay replied.

"Then I shall write and tell her of what she needs to know, at least part of it. She does not need to be burdened with all of this sorry tale just yet," Lady de Mandeville sighed.

"Is the general found then?" Harry asked.

"Found, and gone missing again. Well, missing as far as any authority, and Fitzwilliam, are concerned. He will reach our compound

within the month, and then we shall know

everything," Lady de Mandeville replied.

"Good, he deserves all the evil that will

befall him," Captain Finlay said.

"Indeed, though this whole business is a

sorry state of affairs. Sarah has become far more

involved than I ever wished her to be. Had it

been that we had just recovered the pocket

watch in the first place, she would have been

spared all of this, but now. Now she is in far

deeper than she realises and the danger she

faces is immeasurable," Lady de Mandeville

said, shaking her head with regret.

"You sound as though you are speaking

of your daughter," Harry said with a frown.

"Not my daughter, she is far more dear to

me than that. She is one of the few that seems able to play on this grand stage. I do not deny I would have her spared the danger, but look at all the good she has done," the countess replied.

"Can anything be done to prevent further harm to her?" Captain Finlay asked, already expecting the answer.

"Killing Fitzwilliam, but even then there would be another, and another. It does not end," Lady de Mandeville sighed.

Lady Sarah recovered from her poisoning somewhat more slowly than she would have liked. The exercising of the horses and her other duties around the manor were all taken up by Sylvia until her mistress was recovered.

With the danger passed, and the knowledge that Lady Sarah would live, all of the guests who had travelled to attend the engagement party of the pair departed to return to their homes.

Baron von Stockmar related the tale in full to Queen Victoria and Prince Albert, and the queen's family had their own spin on the story that was circulated around court for many months after.

The Evans family stayed a day or two longer to visit with Arwyn before they had to return home to Wales, but there were plans for another engagement to take place once the wedding of Lady Sarah and Mr Hunter had been held.

Mr Christian and Mr Claydon came to drink and share stories with the brigadier and the doctor and to help keep watch over the house for a few nights after all the guests had left, and Mrs Claydon came to play bridge in the library with Sylvia, Lady Sarah and Mr Hunter.

The Duke of Wellington and Charles Arbuthnot returned home once the former diplomat was satisfied nothing more could be learned, and left the locating of the general in the hands of the police and foreign office.

It was a week after the departure of all their friends, that Lady Sarah received the letter from Lady de Mandeville. It read:

Dearest Sarah

I must apologise for the position you have been placed in. For now, I would have you know how deeply I regret the necessity of your involvement, but there will come a day when I hope that you can escape from it.

The name behind the general is Fitzwilliam, and though the police will fear he has slipped their net and gone to ground, and the foreign office will fear he has gotten away to the shores of another land, please rest assured that he has done neither of these things, and is presently being most accommodating with information. I leave London today to return home, though I shall be back for your wedding.

There is a great deal more I would tell you, but now is not the time, and a letter is not the place. Until I see you again, stay well, and eat plenty of fish and meat. I am told that the vitamin in it is very good for you,

Your devoted friend

Carol-Ann

There was much in the letter that she did not understand, but a great deal of the information contained within it did make her smile. Knowing that the general was in her custody did make her feel a good deal better. But she knew there would be other agents, and other dangers yet to face.

As she grew stronger, the villagers of Stickleback Hollow organised a small celebration that was held at Wilson's inn. It was not small for the number of guests that attended as the whole village attended, but it was nothing more than a few drinks and a few platters of food that Emma put on. That is until people started bringing food out of their houses and from the manor house.

It lasted late into the night and by the end of it, only Lady Sarah, Mr Hunter and Mr Brown remained standing.

"There is one thing I shall say for this place, they do know how to celebrate," Mr

Brown said with wry amusement as he looked over the people who had passed out at the tables in the inn.

"They are well practised in it, for certain," Mr Hunter replied.

"I know we haven't always had the easiest of friendships, but I feel now that is as good a time as any to finally bury the hatchet between us. I meant what I said, that I would be your friend no matter who it was you chose, and I would like it if you and I could be friends as well, Alexander," Mr Brown said as he held out his hand to the son of the brigadier.

"I would like that too, perhaps we can be like my father and the doctor, in time," Mr Hunter said as he accepted the offered hand.

"In time, perhaps we shall, but for now I

am happy enough to say congratulations to you both, and I truly wish you a world of happiness," Mr Brown said.

Love the book? Need to know what's next in Stickleback Hollow?

A love of music, death threats to a Prima Donna, and a clever Lady on the case. Will A Night at the Opera turn deadly?

Get *A Night at the Opera* now!

Want to stay up-to-date on the latest news from my books? Want to get access to pre-order discounts and the chance to be part of my Advanced Reader and Street Teams? Then sign up for my newsletter here!

Looking for more than just books? You can get the latest releases from me, signed paperbacks and hardbacks, mugs, t-shirts, journals as well as books and digital bundles from

https://www.cswoolley.com

Love the Mysteries of Stickleback Hollow? Not caught up with the rest of the series, then jump back to *A Thief in Stickleback Hollow*, Book 1 in the Mysteries of Stickleback Hollow and see how it all began.

Want to help a reader out? Reviews are crucial when it comes to helping readers choose their next book and you can help them by leaving just a few sentences about this book as a review. It doesn't have to be anything fancy, just what you liked about the book and who you think might like to read it. **Scan the QR Code below or visit**

https://mybook.to/EngagementStickleback

If you don't have time to leave a review or don't feel confident writing one, recommending a book to your family, friends and co-workers can help them choose their next book, so feel free to spread the word.

Historical Note

In the 18th Century, Bourbon Whiskey was born. How it came to be is a matter of much contention as it's creation is not well documented, but it has existed for several centuries. What is certain is that it became known as Bourbon in the 1850s and was not known as Kentucky Bourbon until the 1870s.

Bourbon differs from whisky in a number of ways, and not simply in the spelling. Whiskey and Whisky are not the same drink. Whisky refers to those beverages produced in Scotland, Canada and Japan, where as Bourbon can only be produced in the United States. Bourbon must be made from at least 51% corn and distilled at 80% and aged in new oak barrels. Whisky, by comparison does not use new barrels, but old barrels, and in many cases, old bourbon barrels to age. There is also no corn involved in the creation of Whisky, instead it is made using malted barley.

Scotch Whisky can only be produced in Scotland. But, to my early point, Whiskey is a product of Ireland and the United States. Bourbon may fall under the Whiskey bracket, but not all Whiskies (the plural is the same confusingly) produced in the United States are automatically bourbon.

Whiskey created in Ireland is made from

malted barley but rather than being distilled twice, as in Scotland, Canada and Japan, it is distilled three times.

Finally, to complete your very brief education in the different hard spirits that often fall under the Whiskies heading, there is Rye. Rye is made from at least 51% rye grain and it has a different distillation process.

Whisky comes from Gaelic and translates as "water of life". If you had not guessed by this point, I am a whisky drinker, though I had found a bourbon I like (Buffalo Trace) and I do enjoy an Irish Whiskey on occasion, I am predominately a fan of Single Malt whisky. Not only is it a wonderful drink to enjoy on an evening of mulling over ideas and warming the heart, but it is very useful in the combating of chest infections, throat infections and flu. During the three times I contracted COVID-19 (and yes, I was vaccinated, I just have asthma which places me at greater risk of infections that attack the lungs) whisky was one of the few things that kept me going - along side Maxagesic PE and Codral syrup.

Mr Charles Charnley was the inspiration for the character of Mr Charnley in Chester. He was the chemist of my home town of Wilmslow in Cheshire, and was a Victorian chemist at that. If you do a brief search for him, you will find photographs and records of his prescriptions dating back to 1866. He was not the most reputable chemist in Chester, but his reputation was such in Wilmslow that his shop lasted from 1864 until 2008.

I can remember as a child going to Charnley's on a regular basis to collect medicine, for the chemist to look at minor injuries or ailments that were not worth the wait at the doctor's surgery. The interior was very much unchanged since the time of it's opening and was a wonder in dark woods and glass, with a raised counter and a feeling of permanence. In Victorian England the most popular poison was arsenic, it was used in pretty much everything you can think of and it was an easy poison to disguise the effects of since the primary symptoms of arsenic poisoning are vomiting and diarrhoea - something that many illnesses of the time had in common with the poison.

Like arsenic, strychnine and cyanide were widely available. You could go to your local chemist and collect the three poisons in the same afternoon. They were sold as rat poisons or other pesticides, and most people never thought much of using them on their friends and neighbours. Of the three, cyanide was one a poison that would very plainly indicate murder, and the reason it was chosen for this particular story - namely Fitzwilliam wanted Lady Sarah's death to be known for what it was, and let fear do the rest.

It is possible to survive all three poisons

depend on the dosage, your health and a few

other factors, though all three require

immediate medical attention should you find

yourself suffering any of the associated

symptoms. One of he treatments for cyanide

poisoning involves using a created form of the

vitamin B12 which binds with the cyanide in

the system and helps the liver deal with the

poison (it's a lot more complicated than that,

but that seems to be the general idea behind it).

So when it is suggested that Lady Sarah eat

plenty of fish and meat, it is because they are

rich in B12!

You may be wondering why methylene blue is

not mentioned in this book, and that is because

it was not created until 1876, and it was not used successful for cyanide poisoning until 1926! So even by my standards of moving history around by a decade or two, having methylene blue involved would be a step too far.

The press is not something that I have focused too much on in these stories, and how they would undoubtedly becoming more interested in Lady Sarah's exploits, do not worry, the days where her name makes headlines are coming, and the reason for the absence will be revealed, though the more canny amongst you may already have some theories about why her name has been kept, rather surreptitiously, from becoming a household name. You'll find out if you were right in a few volumes time!

Lady Sarah was taken to hospital in Manchester, and those of you that have read A Thief in Stickleback Hollow, might recall that the particular hospital in question was founded in 1752 as a cottage hospital caring for 12 patients by Joseph Bancroft, a local industrialist, and Charles White, a surgeon. By 1755 the hospital had grown and need larger premises, so it was moved to the site where Piccadilly Gardens now stand.

In 1763 a lunatic asylum was added to the hospital, though this was moved to Cheadle in Cheshire in 1849. In 1791 a library was added to the hospital. The hospital was originally known as the Manchester Infirmary, but was renamed the Manchester Royal Infirmary in 1830. In 1908 the hospital was moved from the Piccadilly Gardens site to its current location on Oxford Road after concerns were raised about evacuation in the event of a fire.

What you will not know is that I had considered using the Ancoats Hospital as the hospital in both A Thief in Stickleback Hollow and this book. The reason I considered using Ancoats is that my grandmother worked as a nurse there when she was young. The painting by Lowry of the outpatient waiting room, well a print of it, hangs in her living room because she remembers so much from her time working there with great fondness. She remembers the name of the porter who worked in the little glass booth at the far end of the hall depicted in the painting. However, Ancoats was a hospital that was set up, originally, as a charity for the middle class and working class residents of the Ancoats area and those areas beyond.

It was originally the Ardwick and Ancoats Dispensary and it did not seem appropriate for Lady Sarah to be a patient there. The dispensary was originally conceived to help alleviate some of the pressures on the Manchester Infirmary. Salford and Chorlton-on-Medlock also had their own dispensaries. As Manchester Infirmary was run on the basis of subscriptions, it also made sense that the wealthy members of Grangeback Manor would have paid for the privilege of using the facilities there as well as those available in Chester.

In this book, the exploits of the Duke of Wellington are alluded to but never mention in full, so here are a few career highlights of which he can boast. The Duke of Wellington (and his allies) defeated Napoleon at the battle of Waterloo. He won numerous strategic battles in France, Spain and India. He was given the nickname, the Iron Duke. If you want to see an enjoyable telling of the exploits of Wellington, I can recommend the television series Sharpe, starring Sean Bean (a very young and rakish Sean Bean) as Sharpe, one of Wellington's soldiers as they campaign across Europe, beating back Napoleon. It is based on the book series by Bernard Cornwell (which I also recommend), and there are a number of famous and well-loved faces you will recognise in the TV series.

About the Author

I was born in Macclesfield, Cheshire, UK, and raised in the nearby town of Wilmslow. From an early age, I discovered I had a flair and passion for writing.

I began writing at the age of 7 and was first published in 2010. I currently live with my partner, Matt, and our two cats in Christchurch, New Zealand.

As an avid horsewoman and gamer, I also have a passion for singing, dancing, the theatre, and my garden.

Facebook:

https://www.facebook.com/AuthorC.S.Woolle
y

Instagram:

https://www.instagram.com/thecswoolley

Website: http://www.cswoolley.com

Acknowledgements

Writing can be an extremely lonely profession at times, but thankfully I never have to go through any of the pressures alone. My wonderful Matthew has been a source of constant support to me during all of my writing endeavours since we first met. I couldn't ask for a more fitting partner to share my life or love with.

Writing is not something I stumbled into either, my mother, Helen, took me, and my sisters, to the library every weekend when we were young to get different books, and I always maxed out the number of books I could get. Not only did she encourage me to read, but to write as well. To say I have been writing stories and poetry since I was 7 is not an exaggeration and the development of my writing career is due in no small part to her.

My mother-in-law, Lesley, has also been a source of unflinching and unwavering support, something I could not do without.

To Laura and Sam, who have read and offered opinions, death threats and encouragement on my early drafts, you are true treasures. Amy, you too are worth your weight and more in gold for all your love and support.

It may seem that writers only function alone,

but I am blessed to be part of an amazing community of authors whom I know who have helped push me to even greater heights and success. For the last few months I have relied on a small group of friends more than most, my dearest Victoria Tait, Glenn Salter, Jacqui Penn, Theresa Papa, Michelle Nelson-Schmidt, and Chez Churton, my dear friends, thank you.

And finally, to you, dear reader, without you there would be no books, no series, no career. I want to thank you for all the time that you spend reading my work, reviewing it, and sharing it with your friends and family. Without you, there would be nothing. Thank you from the bottom of my heart.

Until we meet again in my next book, thank you and adieu.